THE ANGEL

A TRIBUTE TO "THE DYING CHILD"

TROY LAMBERT

PART THE FIRST

Here's so cold, and winds outside are frightening,

But in dreams--ah, that's what I like best:

I can see the darling angel children,

When I shut my sleepy eyes and rest.

Hans Christian Anderson, "The Dying Child"

ABEL

THUMP-STEP.

T*hump-step.*

How he hates that sound! The sound of crutch striking against stone! The cobbles make to trip him but he resists with what little balance and strength he has. There a lamppost! A resting place created by the city for beggars such as he.

The clattering of wagon wheels interrupts his heavy breathing. A noble man it is indeed who rushes by with such fine horses and iron clad wheels. His passage wakes the city.

An old dog barks. Also a cripple and a beggar, the dog often competes with him for meager scraps. He ignores the animal. At the present his interests lay not with his stomach but in an empty lot ahead. Debris covers the place where a fine building once stood. It burned to the ground last winter. The ashes of the once majestic structure now hold a rare sight of beauty in this landscape so blighted by humanity. In the ash enriched soil sprouts a flower garden. Every day he can manage he tends the flowers.

Thistles and weeds attempt to raise their heads and he strikes them down, killing them with reckless abandon. Nearby he found a discarded miner's pick. When he cannot pluck the weeds with his weak arms he uses it to tear them from the earth..

As he rounds the corner a fit of coughing doubles him over. He leans on another strategic lamppost and closes his eyes.

Medicine served up in dreams heals his ruined frame but he wakens daily to the reality of his life. A runaway from the orphanage where the headmaster touched all the boys in unpleasant ways and continued to receive payment from the Baron anyway, the streets became his home and the stray dogs his family. The other beggars became his competition.

He learned the harsh rules of street life. He walked without fear, ate with regularity that made others jealous, and even shared when he could. He kept only one thing completely to himself. This flower garden.

On a Thursday he saw the doctor walking home. In his arms he held a bundle of flowers bought from the market. An idea bloomed.

There's no harm in trying, he thought.

"Drink this."

The taste assaults his tongue and bruises it worse than the rotgut wine the older beggars make in barrels under the bridge.

"You're a sick young man."

He nods.

"Where are your parents?"

"Ain't got any."

"You don't have any. At least speak properly."

"Yes sir."

"Why do you not live at the orphanage?"

He shrugs.

"Never mind. I see the sores and bruises of those boys. Better to roam the streets than to suffer the hand of Olaf, eh?"

He nods. The doctor corrected his poor speech so strictly he fears to utter an answer that might bring an end to his treatment.

"Where did you get the flowers?"

He shrugs again.

"You didn't steal them?"

A head shake.

"No matter then. They please my wife. I'm going to give you this." He writes in a beautiful script on a piece of precious paper. "It'll help with your cough. Stay away from sleeping near the river. Drink water from the fountains when you can. Come back next Thursday with more flowers and I'll check on you again."

"Thank you sir, but I can't pay the druggist."

"Tell him to place it to my charge. Here, let me write it for you." He scribbles again and holds the paper out.

The beggar takes it. "Thank you sir. I ain't. . .you're very kind."

The doctor tussles his hair as a father would a son's. "See you next week."

Afraid, he doesn't go to the pharmacy the first week. The second week he does. The third he feels a little better.

* * *

He leans against the lamppost once more and looks at his dying garden. He shakes the brown bottle and looks at the tiny amount of liquid remaining there. His forehead burns with fever and he doesn't see the doctor until tomorrow.

The flowers wilt. The heat beats down on them day after day. He brings water when he can. Opens the dying petals and scatters seeds over the rich soil. The sun shines too strong without the shadow of clouds or rain.

"Driest summer in decades," he hears the old men say.

He toils on. Flowers serve as currency. Until last week he felt much better.

Thursday on his way downtown after delivering flowers and seeing the doctor he saw the dog standing on his hind legs digging through the trash behind the bakery.

Bread, he thought. Energy giving bread. Even days old and dry and covered with mold, bread fills his belly like nothing else. Pocketing the brown bottle of medicine he walked over. The dog eyed him and growled. Not an entirely uncommon situation.

He reached for a stale loaf to call his own, and the dog bit him.

He howled in pain. Blood welled up where teeth punctured the skin. He dropped the bread and backed away. The dog kept munching away.

The next night he struck the dog with his crutch while it slept. It whimpered and ran away. It seemed now that the dog would have the last laugh after all.

He looks at his hand. Red and swollen, six fat lines run up his arm from the teeth marks. Monday the fever struck. Tuesday it got better, today worse again. The red lines thicken, the swelling threatens to split his skin.

The bucket sloshes against his bad leg as he limps across the lot. Spread seeds. Water the flowers. Pink, red, yellow, orange. Once open to the sky, their heads now bow low.

He finds himself on his hands and knees, head swimming, pain unbearable. He plucks the best of the pitiful plants and struggles to his feet. He will go see the doctor a day early.

He staggers from post to post, sweat stinging his eyes, the crutch and his bad leg a constant hindrance.

Staggers up the steps and strikes the door as hard as his weakened condition allows. The doctor's wife responds to the timid tapping.

He sways, holding out the flowers. She snatches them from his trembling hand.

"Come quickly Ham! It's the boy!" He hears her call out to her husband, and then he falls face first into their home.

ZACH

Mom pulls the stocking hat down over my bald head, and pats me on the shoulder. She cries a lot.

I have cancer and there's nothing I can do about it. Mom and dad try to tell me it's okay, but I hear them at night, and I have a computer. I'm smart for my age, and I know my chances.

Not good. Most of my friends talk about what they want to be when they grow up. Firemen, policemen, miners, doctors, vets. I don't think I will ever grow up so I'm trying to make the most of every day. *If* I grow up I want to be an angel.

Dad honks the horn and I grab my skis. My legs are really tired, but I don't want to tell him. I want to ski today until I can't any more. Any time he offers to take me, I go with my dad. Mom worries but he argues with her. After all, what could the harm be? Either I die doing something I want to do, or I just die.

Death isn't scary to me. I already see the angels. They talk to me from time to time. Usually it's when I'm in the hospital and the doctors are giving me the special drugs or an I.V. of some sort. I know what the stuff does, even if they don't want me to.

The medicine kills cells. Most of the time it kills the cells they want it to, or at least tries to stunt their growth. It kills good cells too, the stuff that makes up me. I'm Zach, I'm twelve, and they tell me I am very brave. I don't feel brave though. I feel scared.

I'm dying. I don't know when. But today I'm going skiing with my dad.

* * *

I t's called a terrain park, but it's not really terrain. At least that's what dad says. Man-made obstacles aren't really terrain at all. They're anti-terrain. He comes in here with me because he loves me. He even learned to slide rails and do the C-box. The thing my dad is good at is the jumps. Big air. Even though the tricks he does are pretty old, I still cheer.

He's coming over the jump now, and I hold the video camera as steady as I can. My hands are starting to shake, and I know I've pushed myself too hard. It's time to go in and rest my body. Get something to eat, hydrate a bit. What I really need is to go home but I don't want this day to be over.

He flies over the lip into view and does a simple 180, landing backwards. He skis up to me and spins around.

"How you feeling Zach?"

"I'm okay."

"I think we should go in kiddo."

"One more run."

"Z-man. . ."

"Please dad."

He can't tell me no. We ski to the lift and head up one more time.

At the top I see the familiar sign. "6500 feet." I love the mountain top, but I can hardly breathe now. One more run will be plenty for the day.

"Ready?" Dad asks.

"Race you down!" I take off. I skate a little at first to get some speed, even though I know he'll catch up to me.

The wind whips past me. My vision starts to blur, and I can't get enough air into my lungs. I try to cry out, but I feel the world tilting as I fall over. I feel my skis release and I leave them behind on the snow. I drop my poles too, and hear dad laughing. He thinks it's just one of my famous "Zach yard sale" crashes.

The sky twirls in my goggle distorted vision as I spin down the hill on my back unable to control myself. I slide for a really long time.

I finally stop, and I feel air gradually coming back into my lungs. Nothing hurts. I try to sit up, but I just don't have the strength. My head gets a few inches off the snow and then drops back.

Dad's face enters my vision, and his smile falters.

"Zach?"

I try to answer him, but I can hardly breathe. "Tired," I finally manage.

"Okay. I'm gonna get us some help."

He starts to shout and wave, and some other people ski over. Dad is here. It's going to be okay. So I rest.

* * *

There is music. Sweet music. An angel is beside me.

"Is it time?" I ask.

"Not yet."

"It feels so good here."

"Your mother and father need you a bit longer."

"It feels good to rest."

He kisses me on the cheek. His wings brush my face as he turns to leave.

"Take me with you."

He keeps walking and doesn't answer.

* * *

"No more skiing."

"But he loves to ski."

"You heard the doctor. It's just too risky."

"It's what he wants to do."

"He's dying Rick!"

"You think I don't know that? He's my son too."

"No more skiing," I say from the bed. It's not the first time I've heard them argue and I doubt they will stay together when I'm gone. I've read the books and I know their odds too. Life after death is hard even on earth.

"Z-man." He shoots her a dirty look that he thinks I don't see.

"Seasons almost over dad, and I want to see the flowers."

"Flowers?'

"Remember that place we went to in California? All the flowers?"

"The one in Mendocino?"

"Yeah. I want to go there."

"Why buddy?"

"I want to see spring again."

"You will." My mom starts to cry.

"How much time do I have left dad?"

"What do you mean? You have your whole life ahead of you."

"Dad."

He puts his head down sobbing. I start to tear up too, but I have to be strong for them. For me too, but mostly for them.

"Mom?"

She looks away. I grab my father's hand. "Daddy."

He looks up, the tears stopping. He wants to be strong for me and mom too, I can tell.

"A month buddy. Maybe six weeks. Unless a miracle happens."

"Okay." I feel sobs rising in my twelve year old chest, but I can't cry now. Not now.

"I'm done with school," I say. "I want to go see spring." Besides skiing, spring is my favorite time of year. It's only March in North Idaho though, and spring could be a long way away.

"Okay." Dad pats my arm, and mom sobs and runs out of the room. He looks after her. "She'll be okay, Z-man."

"Dad, I may be only 12, but I'm not stupid. Try to stay with her when I'm gone. She's gonna be a mess for a while. I'm gonna be fine."

"Buddy. . ."

"Dad, I'll be with the angels, watching."

"Son, it's not that simple."

"Promise me you'll try dad."

"Okay."

"Promise."

So he did. He promised me he would try. Really, what more could ask of him?

ABEL

He lies on the bed, ice soaked cloths pressed to his burning forehead from time to time. He sits up and coughs. A hand grips the back of his neck, and helps him remain upright. Sweet cold water touches his lips and he swallows eagerly. A second later, a shot of brandy follows. Sweet brandy not like the stuff he's tasted on the streets.

He can't afford this. He knows he can't. Someone is giving it to him anyway. He swallows a fire that slides down to his belly and seems uncertain if it wants to stay. He tries to move his right hand, and it seems lighter than before. A throbbing pain slithers up his arm to the shoulder. He turns his head that direction but the hand behind his neck prevents him from going too far.

"Ham!" The familiar voice of the doctor's wife calls out. "He's awake! He's awake! Come quickly!"

His head spins and when she lets his neck go his head falls recklessly back to the rough linen below. He closes his eyes, and on the inside of his eyelids a bright and blinding light shines. He tries to open them, but can't.

An imposing form materializes. Two snow-white wings sprout from its back. "Fear not." The bass of its voice vibrates his every nerve.

"You're an angel."

"How do you know?"

"Angels always say that first."

"Indeed we do. But yours are a fearful people."

"Am I dead?"

"Not yet. It is not yet time."

"I'm so cold."

The figure turns and walks away. He calls after it, but no answer comes. He feels hands slap his face then, rough hands shake his shoulders, and sound fills his world.

"Boy! Boy! Wake up! Wake up!"

Icy water cascades over his body, and he jumps but remains unable to reply. He feels strong hands lift his too light form, and a moment later he's immersed in icy water. It seems to turn to steam as it flashes onto his forehead.

It feels good. He eases into consciousness. The doctor's face is close to his and real candles burn in the background. Also in the background stands a winged figure that moves from shadow to shadow, visible by its dispelling of darkness. No one else seems to notice it.

* * *

Hours flee the day. He murmurs in and out of sleep. He dreams of angel kisses and winged flight. He fades in and out of a room flickering with candle light and people keeping watch over him. From time to time he hears them speaking of someone that must be him.

"The fever can't go any higher."

"Will he live?"

"He burns like a furnace."

"Nay, like a sun."

"Aye, the July sun."

Later: "He talks as he sleeps."

"Of what does he speak?"

"Of angels. Is the priest ready?"

"I pray we will have no need of him."

"Pray if you will. I will watch and call *when* we have need of him."

These speakers dressed in the yin and yang habits of the One True Church. He's not a believer, although his mother named him after the first son of Adam and Eve.

He sees the angels. The nuns don't, or at least they don't acknowledge them. He wonders how true their belief is.

He rises to the surface of consciousness once more. He sits up on his own, feeling oddly strong and better.

* * *

It takes the doctor a long time to come. He realizes he's no longer at the doctor's home. The convent he imagines or the home the Church runs for the urchins. He doesn't care which he just wants to drop back into sleep.

"Stay with us," one says.

"It is a miracle you live at all!" The second nun crosses herself and bows her head.

"What do you mean?" He manages a whisper.

"The doctor will explain," the eldest of them states. They speak no more.

Time passes slowly. The doctor arrives. He waves the nuns from the room. "Abel, is it?"

"That's my name."

"It is better I call you that than 'boy.'"

He smiles.

"Able the dog was sick."

"So he made me sick. Or sicker."

A nod.

"Will I die?"

"I don't know."

"My hand?"

"Gone."

"Gone?"

The doctor lifts his injured arm and brings it into his sight. Abel feels him grab his hand, but when he looks there's nothing below his elbow.

For a moment he sobs. His eyes leak no water as his body is as dry as ashes. "Did you catch the bite in time?"

The doctor shakes his head, and Abel sees the tears standing in the corner of his eyes.

"Is that why I may not live?"

"Abel, I don't understand why you're this awake. You aren't getting better except. . ."

"The nuns mentioned a miracle."

"It's your only hope."

He looks again at where his arm should be, and down at his crippled leg. "I match."

"You match?"

"Bad hand. Bad leg. If I live, I match."

"I see."

"I want to sleep."

"I know. Do you pray?"

"No."

"Me either. If you were to take it up though, now would be the time."

"I may." He closes his eyes, and far away a winged figure walks toward him with deliberate steps.

The doctor watches as his chest rises and falls with increasing speed. A moment later, it stops. One last sigh escapes the lips of the beggar boy and rises to the celling, taking with it his soul. He speaks a word to a God he doesn't believe in, asking that God to take the boy's soul, if he's there at all.

From his mouth to the ears of God. . .

* * *

To the lips of an angel. The angel leans over the boy and kisses him on the cheek. A form rises after the kiss, hovering over the boy and forming a new body, one with no limp and a whole arm. From the back of the figure sprout two wings. In moments they grow and mature.

"Where am I?"

"You are among the angels."

"I'm dead?"

"Your earthly life is over."

"What next then?"

"Follow me."

"What will I do?"

"You will tend the flower gardens of heaven."

Abel smiles and takes the hand of his new companion. Together they walk a few blocks. Abel wants to take a few flowers with him. Flowers he himself had planted on earth. The angel waits as he navigates the debris of the empty lot and gathers a few blossoms.

ZACH

The ribbon of the road unwound under the car. My parents took me to California. In Mendocino I saw rhododendrons, fuchsias, magnolias, azaleas, camellias, and a multitude of flowering shrubs. We walked over trails and bridges that forded streams. We walked through fern covered canyons, and when I could walk no more, my father carried me.

We spent seven days in the gardens of Golden State Park. My father bought me a tiny camera, and I took hundreds of pictures of the daffodils surrounding the Dutch Windmills and the cherry trees blooming in the Japanese Tea Garden. Near the end, my father rented a wheelchair and tirelessly wheeled me from place to place.

Mother often stayed behind in the hotel room. She avoided eye contact with me, and hardly looked at my father. She drank and thought I did not see or know. The vodka bottles came and went with the bottles of Listerine and the gum she popped between her teeth. As I got sicker and weaker, so did she.

In a restaurant on Fisherman's Wharf I realized I couldn't go on any longer. You know the place, where they dump the seafood all over your table? I couldn't even crack my own crab legs. I sat back in the wheelchair that seemed my last home.

"Tomorrow we head down the coast."

"Dad, I can't." My breath came in ragged gasps. I felt dizzy.

"Buddy, sure you can."

"It's time Dad. I need to rest."

"But you wanted. . ."

"I know."

He cried for the first time then. The rest of the meal he opened shells and fed me what little I could eat. We got back to the room and mom took one look at me and started to cry.

"How is he?"

Dad shook his head.

Mom came over and hugged me tighter than she had in weeks. Even when I started to squirm she wouldn't let go. I wouldn't have squirmed as much if I had known. I swear I wouldn't have.

My dad called University of California San Francisco Helen Diller Family Comprehensive Cancer Center. It sounded hopeful and peaceful. They offered to see me in the morning.

Mom and Dad both tucked me in. I fell into sleep immediately after I told them I loved them.

* * *

It was dark in the room but light came from the corner. I sat straight up, not remembering a night light there before. There wasn't. An angel stood quietly looking at me. He blinked and a tear rolled down his cheek.

"Time?"

He did not answer. He simply crossed the room and kissed my cheek. Suddenly I was standing and felt better than I had in weeks. I felt something rising from my shoulders, adding new weight there. I looked right and left. Beautiful white wings that resembled those of the apparition before me appeared. A feather from one fell out and onto the floor.

"Come with me."

"What will we do?"

"Gather flowers from earth for the gardens of heaven. Then you can help me tend them if you wish."

"Is it spring there?"

"It's always spring there. Always winter, always fall, always summer. There is no time, no seasons."

I smiled and took his hand. "Can we do one thing first?"

"Certainly." It was as if he already knew.

* * *

The scream woke Zach's father. He bolted up right and ran to Zach's room in the suite. His mother completely covered the boy's small body. She was kissing the face over and over.

She sat up and pulled the lifeless head into her lap.

"No, no, no," she rocked back and forth. "My boy, my boy."

Zach's father dialed 9 and then 1 on his phone. Realizing the futility of the action, he hung up. Zach was gone.

"Promise me." His son's voice reminded him.

He went to her, and put his arms around her. He held her for what seemed like a long time. She laid the body gently back on the bed.

"Who should we call?"

He shrugged, not knowing the answer. He offered her his hand, and they closed the door quietly as if fearing their boy might wake. They stepped into the central room and both gasped at the same time.

The coffee table was filled with flowers. Flowers in the most beautiful crystal vases they had ever seen.

Zach's father dialed the operator with one hand, and held his wife with the other. From far away Zach watched, a tear rolling down his cheek.

"Will they be okay?"

"I don't know."

"I thought there was no crying in heaven."

"We aren't there yet."

"When will we get there?"

"Soon. We have work first." In his hands he held two empty baskets. He handed one to Zach.

Zach looked at it and smiled. "For flowers?"

The angel nodded.

"Where will we start?"

A hand clapped him on the back. "Close by my friend."

PART I

PART THE SECOND

Mother, look, the Angel's here beside me!

Listen, too, how sweet the music grows.

See, his wings are both so white and lovely;

Surely it was God who gave him those.

Green and red and yellow floating round me,

They are flowers the Angel came and spread.

Shall I, too, have wings while I'm alive, or--

Mother, is it only when I'm dead?

Hans Christian Anderson, "The Dying Child"

ABEL AND ZACH

High over the world they flew. They traveled at speeds Zach would have thought impossible. Places they visited were those he once only dreamed of. The greatest gardens of the world were his for the choosing. From roses and tulips to the most exotic of flowers and blooms he touched and plucked them all.

In Portland, Oregon they stopped at the Test gardens and gathered roses of every shape and color. Red, pink, yellow, white, and even a rare purple. They flew through the Sculpture Gardens of Minnesota. Spring shouldn't have arrived, but it had, and they plucked the best of the cherry blossoms there.

At Butchart Gardens in British Columbia daffodils of every color fell into their baskets and should have filled them, but they did not. The baskets seemed bottomless. The fragrance that rose from the fallen flowers filled their senses with a blend of perfumes never envisioned by man.

Sunsets blended into sunrise. Oranges, reds, pinks decorated first the East and then the West. Day fled into day, night into night. Around the world they spun, seeking the best the earth had to offer. They gathered creations for the creator.

In Japan they skimmed over the peaceful ponds in Rikugien Garden. From the Himeji Castle Garden they plucked daises and sunflowers by the dozens. They gathered orchids from Singapore, tulips form the Netherlands, and poppies from Flanders fields in Belgium. When it seemed the basket and his eyes could hold no more Abel beckoned to him.

"It is time for you to see the greatest garden."

"Truly? There are gardens greater than what we have seen?"

"Only one."

* * *

They hovered over the central part of Europe. Time seemed to slide backward under their feet, a thing Zach once thought impossible.

The streets below them ran dirty with sewage. Horses and buggies hurried to and fro. In the midst sat a small group of beggar boys. The largest of them moved to club the smallest on the ear, but his hand stopped in mid swing as though he sensed their presence.

"Where are we?"

Abel only smiled and pointed down the street. Zach's feet touched the dirty cobbles and he began to walk. No beauty grew here, only pain and sadness. He looked back at Abel, who only gestured for him to go on.

He rounded a corner and if he'd not been an angel a carriage would have run him down. Zach still found it odd to be somewhere and yet not be there. As he paused and looked at the driver, the carriage slowed. The noble in the back tossed a shilling from his pocket at the foot of a beggar boy who stood at the corner, leaning on a crutch. Zach recognized Abel.

A moment later the boy vanished and the angel stood in his place. "Abel?"

"Sometimes we can be what we once were, for a time."

"I don't understand."

"You have much to learn. Halfway down the block you will find what you are looking for."

Zach walked on. An old building was nearly falling into the street. He rounded the corner and saw before him and empty lot. In the center a thin row of flowers grew. They were of no species he knew from their travels. Speechless he crossed the lot and kneeled in the dirt beside them.

"Go ahead pick a few, but only a few." Abel stood at his shoulder, his voice choked with tears.

"What is this place?"

"It was once my garden. My hope."

Zach looked up and saw before him once again the crippled beggar boy with the crutch. Tears stood in his eyes.

"This is where the angel, my angel took me from."

"You died here?"

"Not far away. I plucked my last flowers from this place. I still come to tend it when I can."

"What do you mean your angel?'

"One came to me, as I came to you."

"What did you do then?"

"I gathered flowers from earth for the gardens of heaven."

"But then?"

"I tend those gardens still."

"Yet you came for me."

"From time to time, I must be someone's angel. As my angel came for me."

"What now?"

Abel smiled. They rose through the clouds and suddenly the earth was far below. They whizzed past the red ball of Mars, the rings of Saturn and the icy ball known as Pluto so recently demoted to non-planetary status. They left the solar system and flew from the Galaxy, through the Milky Way, and past no longer recognizable constellations. The journey took less time than he would've imagined.

They approached a planet that from above looked much like Earth. A castle appeared in the distance, the sky above it impossibly blue. Its walls glistened like gold, and the colors of the rainbow shown from gems set on the parapets. This, surely this must be heaven.

Abel let go of his hand, and slowly he settled to the ground. He was on a narrow pathway paved in pale metal he assumed was gold. On both sides vast fields of the greatest flowers he had ever seen stretched to the horizon. Many he did not recognize. Bees buzzed from one to the other and somehow he sensed they would never sting him. A large tree stretched for the sky not far away, and under it a lion lay next to a lamb, licking its wool clean with its rough tongue.

Zach moved off the path. "Plant what you have gathered," Abel said, walking away.

Zach surveyed what surrounded him. He saw no weeds. He knelt and ran the soil between his fingers.

Miracle grow, he thought. He giggled.

He glanced back, intending to ask Abel one last question. The angel was gone. In the distance he saw a small boy with a crooked crutch walking toward the golden walls that housed the castle of heaven.

I must go there soon, he thought. *But first these flowers must be planted.*

He got to work, finding open places where the flowers in his basket seemed to fit, to belong, to blend with what already grew there. He smiled as he worked, unaware of any passage of time.

ZACH

A ngels don't need sleep, but sometimes we sleep anyway, at least those of us who were once children. I rarely indulge as there's so much to do, so much to see. I'll never finish it all or even see it all.

"That's what eternity is about," Abel told me last time we crossed paths. "Never bored. Never tiring of things you should never tire of in the first place."

There's no calendar. No need to eat. No bathroom breaks. A perfect place, a perfect world. No crying. No sorrow. I think of my parents from time to time. It doesn't make me sad.

I tend the roses, roses which bare no thorns only the sweetest smelling blossoms. I feel more than see a presence at my elbow.

"Hello Abel."

"Hello Zach. It's time."

"Time for what?"

"Time for you to be someone's angel."

"Return to earth?"

"You must show another what I showed you."

For the first time since entering heaven's gardens, I'm nervous.

* * *

I *wonder if I looked that tiny?*

I look at the boy in the bed below me. His parents flit back and forth. I'm sure mine did too. The boy smiles and reassures them, but I see how his soul clings so feebly to his body. It won't be long.

Flowers decorate the room. They sit on every flat space, in every corner. Vases of rhododendrons, fuchsias, magnolias, azaleas, camellias, and ordinary roses filled the air with fragrance. He stares at me as if he sees me, and I shake my head.

Not time yet. I sense that the time is close.

The door opens and a cart comes in, covered with more flowers. I have no idea where he will put them all, but I smile. On earth, a tear runs down my cheek. I haven't cried since I left, and the tears are of joy this time. Then I see the man pushing the cart as he comes around to shake the hands of the boy's parents.

It's my father. He's older certainly but I recognize the slope of his shoulders, the set of his eyes. He's smiling. A woman enters the room carrying a pitcher of ice water. It's my mother.

I move closer and see on their nametags the words "Children's Hospice." They stayed together. They're helping other parents. I weep for a few moments, and watch as they and the boy's parents embrace and shake hands. The boy simply grins, and my father rubs his rough hand over the boy's bald head just the way he used to do to me.

"You see why you had to come?" Abel asks.

"I see."

"The boy's name is Jack. His dad calls him 'J-man.'"

"When?"

"Tomorrow morning. Tell him tonight."

"Will you stay with me?"

"No. This you must do alone."

"Thanks Abel."

He smiles and fades away.

I look down at Jack and he smiles up at me. I simply nod and smile. It's not yet time.

JACK

I love the flowers and the people who bring them. I've seen the angel. They say I have a chance, but I know better. I'm dying, and soon. The angels don't come until you are close.

I'm not afraid. It's what the angels tell everyone whenever they show up in the Bible. I can't wait to see heaven. I'm not sure my parents believe, but I hope someday they will.

I smile at the angel and he smiles back. A while ago, I saw him crying. Soon I will ask him why.

When? I ask in my mind, hoping he will hear.

Tomorrow morning. He tells me. *Say your goodbyes tonight.*

I cry a little. Not for me. For mom and dad, and those who won't see me anymore.

"J-man."

"Dad."

"Why are you crying? You can still beat this thing."

I know he doesn't believe it. This is hardest on my mother. I shake my head.

"Son, please."

"Dad, I'm dying. It's okay."

He puts his head in his hands.

"Hang in there dad." I'm afraid but I have hope. "I'll be with the angels soon."

"Sure. Stay with us while you can, okay?"

"I love you dad. Send mom in okay? Before you guys leave?"

My mom comes over and I just hug her as tight as I can. She cries, and so do I. I don't want to let her go, but I know I have to. I wave a she leaves, and I wonder if she knows.

I want to think that I will live and I will see them again. But I've seen the angel, and I believe him. I close my eyes, and drift into sleep.

ZACH

"Dad?"

He can't hear me, but seems to sense I'm here. He and my mother hold hands in the waiting room.

"Do you ever feel it?" she asks.

"Feel what?"

"Feel like Zach is. . .here?"

"Like now?"

"Like now."

He pulls him to her. "I do. I really do."

They kiss, and I steal away.

Jack sleeps and I watch from above. It's time. I'm not sure how I know, but I do.

I glide down on my wings, and gently kiss his cheek. He wakes, and his soul leaves his body behind.

I hand him a basket. He takes it from me, and smiles.

"What's your name?"

"I'm Zach."

"Funny, the flower people had a son named Zach who died."

"I know. They're my parents."

"Wow. Does that mean I. . ."

"We'll see. For now, we have work to do."

"What will we do?"

"Gather flowers for the garden of heaven."

"Can we do one thing first?" he asks.

"Sure," I tell him. "Anything at all."

The next morning his mother will awaken to find a vase of the most fragrant flowers she has ever smelled, the most beautiful she has ever seen on the coffee table in their hotel suite.

But we have to hurry if I'm going to get him to the empty lot in time.

Mother, I shall always be with you . . .

Yes, but then you mustn't go on sighing;

When you cry I cry as well, you see.

I'm so tired--my eyes they won't stay open--

Mother--look--the Angel's kissing me

Hans Christian Anderson, "The Dying Child"

47

The End

TL 2013

Harvested is also available in audio format! Find it on Audible and other retailers where you listen to audiobooks.

If you want to join our exclusive review team, see our website for more information. (There is a test, but it's an easy one, I promise!)

In the meantime, be well. More exciting fiction coming soon!

FROM TYPEWRITER REPAIR SHOP: THE BEGINNING

It's funny how you get used to some things. Strange happenings.

Hauntings, if you want to use that word.

I was tired of living in a town where they were almost expected. There wasn't a damn thing anyone in Ridge Falls could do to stop them, at least so it seemed.

So, I bought a house in Garibaldi, a small coastal town in another state. I called it a writer's retreat, a place I'd visit occasionally, but even in the beginning I knew it was more than that. The bay reminded me of the reservoir back home, where the water was both dammed and damned. Held back by a man-made structure, and doomed by the supernatural. Yet, Garibaldi Bay was neither of those things. Their only shared trait was a rolling mist.

But the mists of Garibaldi seemed so innocent in comparison. Eventually, I spent less and less time at "home" and more time at the "retreat."

I remember the day a new storefront appeared in what had been a vacant building downtown because it was also the day I put my home in Ridge Falls on the market. The day I realized Garibaldi was home.

New businesses were uncommon in town, even when they made sense. The rocky piece of Oregon shoreline made tourists bypass this little spot in favor of the white sand beaches of Rockaway or the amusement park atmosphere in Seaside. Only two motels stayed open year round, and were rarely full except for during the annual festival. Other than bars and restaurants, most businesses catered to the commercial fishermen or those employed at the Coast Guard base.

Filling my Jeep at the local gas station, I noticed the "For Rent" sign missing from the dusty window front across the street, and was immediately curious.

"Fill 'er up, Mr. Randall?" the attendant asked. I was adjusting to the Oregon law that required the attendant pump the gas, not the customer.

"You bet, Sam," I said over my shoulder, taking a step toward the street.

"You checkin' out the new shop?" he called after me.

"Thought I might."

"Don't bother. Whoever rented it has a heavy blanket over the front window. Can't see in."

"Any idea who it is?"

"Nope. No one seems to."

"Doesn't Ned's family own the place?"

"Yep. But the guy just told him he needed a store space. Paid a year in advance." Sam spat on the ground, as if disgusted anyone would even try to keep secrets in such a small town.

I shared his disgust that secrecy could be so easily purchased.

In Ridge Falls, secrets ruled.

The pump clicked, and Sam handed me back my credit card. "Thanks," I told him, shaking his hand.

The Jeep started on the first crank, and I made a quick U-turn and headed for home.

ABOUT THE AUTHOR

Troy Lambert is a full-time writer and author. Having written over two dozen mysteries and other novels, Troy is well-versed in story creation, and he knows what it takes to make a fictional story real! Troy's hobbies and pastimes (when he's able to break away from the computer) include hiking into the mountains of Southwest Idaho, fishing in a fast-rushing stream, and going for a drive where his mind can work on creating that perfect twist to the book he's currently writing. A native of Idaho Falls, Idaho, Troy and his wife live in Meridian, Idaho. You can find his other works, including his latest book, *Teaching Moments*, at troylambertwrites.com.

56

THE DOG COMPLEX

Stray Ally

THE "CAPITAL CITY MURDERS" SERIES

"Fast Break"

Book #1 "Overdoses in Olympia"*

Book #2 "Slaying in Salem"*

Book #3 "Strangled in Sacramento"*

Book #4 "deCapitated in Carson City"*

Book #5 "Buried in Boise"*

"The Wicked West"—a compilation of books 1-5, available in both e-books and print*

Book #6 "Hanging in Helena"*

Book #7 "Branded in Bismarck"*

Book #8 "Parricide in Pierre"*

Book #9 "Carnage in Cheyenne"*

Book #10 "Defenestration in Denver"*

"The Nick of Time"—a compilation of books 6-10, available in both e-books and print*

Book #11 "Silenced in Salt Lake"*

Book #12 "Poisoned in Phoenix"*

Book #13 "Stung in Santa Fe"*

Book #14, "Axed in Austin"*

Book #15: "Offered in Oklahoma"*

*These books are now available in audio format!

All the books in the "Capital City Murders" series are available at www.CapitalCityMurders.com and your favorite e-book seller.

www.ingramcontent.com/pod-product-compliance
Lightning Source LLC
Chambersburg PA
CBHW021322160726
47994CB00004B/1574